MALLORY COX AND HIS INTERSTELLAR SOCKS

'Mallory, get those socks off at once before something dangerous happens!'

But Mr Cox's warning came too late. As Mallory crouched down to untie his boot-lace, a beam of violet light shone out of the spacecraft and surrounded him. Mallory suddenly felt as light and bubbly as a milkshake, and before he knew what was happening, he rose gently into the air.

'Hang on tightly, Mallory!' shouted Mr Cox.

'But there's nothing to hang on to!' Mallory wailed.

Dr Topping gave a cry as a second light appeared around him and he too was lifted up towards the glittering spaceship.

'Stand by, dear boy!' bawled Dr Topping. 'I believe they are going to take us on board!'

Mallory Cox and his INTERSTELLAR socks

Andrew Matthews
illustrated by Tony Ross

KNIGHT BOOKS
Hodder and Stoughton

Text copyright © Andrew Matthews, 1992
Illustrations copyright © Tony Ross, 1992

First published in Great Britain in 1992 by J. M. Dent & Sons Ltd.
Knight edition published 1993

British Library C.I.P.

A catalogue record for this book is available from the British Library

ISBN 0 340 58227 8

Printed and bound in Great Britain for Hodder and Stoughton Children's Books, a division of Hodder and Stoughton Ltd., Mill Road, Dunton Green Sevenoaks, Kent TN13 2YA. (Editorial Office: 47 Bedford Square, London WC1B 3DP) by Cox & Wyman Ltd, Reading, Berks.

for David, Jane and Rebecca

-1-

Self-Packing Socks

At the start of the summer holidays, Mallory Cox was in a grumpy mood. Other people in his class at school were jetting off to places like Greece and Florida – but Mallory Cox and his family were going up North to the seaside at Drabthorpe, where they went every year.

"But Drabthorpe is mega-boring!" Mallory complained to his parents. "The town's boring, the beach is boring – it's so boring that the seagulls snore while they're flying because they fall asleep!"

"Nonsense!" Mr Cox replied. "The sea air is bracing and we can go off into the country for long, healthy rambles."

"Huh!" said Mallory, scuffing the toe of his trainers on the living-room carpet. "There isn't anything for me to do in Drabthorpe!"

Mrs Cox, who was busily embroidering a

cushion-cover with a portrait of the royal family, spoke to her son without looking up.

"Why don't you pop upstairs and pack, dear?" she suggested. "Then, when we arrive, you'll have plenty of unpacking to do – and before you know it, it will be time to pack up for coming home again. Packing is the best part of any holiday, I always think."

Mrs Cox held out the cushion-cover at arm's length and squinted. "Embroidery is such an interesting hobby," she declared. "So much more satisfying than origami, or flower-arranging, or rugby! As soon as this cushion-cover is finished, I shall

send it to the Palace. But what a nuisance it is that I've run out of brown thread. The royal corgis will have to be purple!"

Muttering and grumbling to himself, Mallory stumped upstairs to his bedroom and began to pack.

"Drabthorpe is a dump!" he said under his breath. "There's nothing I can do to liven things up. I'll have to sulk a lot and I'll be in a thoroughly bad mood all the time we're there. I'll huff every half-hour and tut every ten minutes, and then I'll . . . a-a-h!"

Mallory said "a-a-h!" because as he lifted a pile of neatly-ironed tee-shirts out of a drawer, he came across his magic socks.

They didn't look magic, they looked like a pair of ordinary, grey socks, but Mallory's witchy Great Aunt Enid had knitted them from the best quality dragon's wool and given them to him as a ninth birthday present. When Mallory put them on, he was liable to have magic doings.

Mr and Mrs Cox disapproved of Mallory's magical footwear and he was not allowed to take them out of the house. The last time he had worn his socks outside, he had been transported back in time and had narrowly escaped being chopped up by a vicious-looking Viking; and the time

before that he had been forced to outrun a seriously hungry, meat-eating dinosaur. Luckily, Mallory was not daunted by such things.

"If the magic socks just happened to get in my suitcase by mistake and I accidentally put them on," Mallory thought aloud, "I might have some interesting adventures, and then Drabthorpe wouldn't be so boring after all. There's just one slight problem . . . "

The slight problem was that when Mallory wore the socks and they started to work, his hair turned all kinds of wild and wonderful colours. If his parents spotted him with a day-glo green hair-do, they would know what he was up to at once.

"Got it!" Mallory exclaimed. "I'll take the balaclava helmet that Granny sent me for Christmas! With that on, you can't even tell if I've got any hair, let alone what colour it is!"

Mallory had stuffed the balaclava at the back of his wardrobe, behind a stack of old *Boffy Facts for Know-it-Alls* magazines and it took a lot of digging to find it. As he was packing the head-gear, Mallory noticed that his magic socks were already in the case – they had jumped in while his back was turned.

"Brilliant!" chuckled Mallory. "Watch out, Drabthorpe, here we come!"

–2–

A Drabthorpe Delicacy

The drive up North was terrible. The roads were more crowded than a turnstile at a World-Cup football final and the Cox family got stuck in one long traffic jam after another.

"Blow and bother!" grumped Mallory, as the car shuddered to a halt yet again. "You might as well start teaching me to drive, Dad. By the time we get to Drabthorpe, I'll be old enough to take my driving test!"

"Don't exaggerate, Mallory," said Mr Cox. "We're only going to be an hour later than we planned . . . or two, or three."

"And besides," Mrs Cox chipped in, "journeys are what holidays are all about. Travelling is such fun!"

"But we're not travelling!" protested Mallory. "We're in the middle of a queue of cars that goes on for miles!"

Mrs Cox seemed not to hear. She examined her embroidery closely and frowned.

"I've just used the last of my pink thread," she said. "I'll have to do the Prince's ears and nose in orange."

It was dark when the Coxes reached The Muddy-view Guest House. They were greeted at the door by the landlady, Mrs Granite, a round woman who always wore a flowery pinafore.

"Ee, it's grand to see you all!" she said. "But you're so late! What kept you?"

"We got held up," Mr Cox explained.

"Ecky thump!" cried Mrs Granite. "Was it a highwayman? I hope he didn't take your buckets and spades!"

She gave Mallory a broad smile that made her face resemble a friendly potato, freshly-peeled.

"My, how you've grown!" she said. "This time last year, you were so small you used to bump your head on the daisies! You've shot up like a runner bean! But you're so skinny, you could slip in under the door if you forgot your key. You need feeding-up, lad, and you've come to the right place for it. Your supper's in the oven, waiting for you."

Even though he hadn't eaten for hours, Mallory clearly remembered what Mrs Granite's cooking

was like from previous years.

"Er . . . gosh, how strange!" he exclaimed. "A fit of not-being-hungry has come over me all of a sudden!"

"We'll soon change that!" cooed Mrs Granite. "Just wait till you see the Drabthorpe delicacy I've got ready for you. A great, steaming plate of marrows stuffed with tripe and minced cow-heel. That's the stuff to stick to your ribs, lad!"

"Aren't we supposed to eat it, then?" Mallory joked feebly.

Mrs Granite paused only to raise an eyebrow at Mallory before leading the way into the dining-room.

The stuffed marrows were worse than the journey. The outside squeaked when Mallory prodded it with his fork and the glistening, grey stuffing kept sliding to the sides of his plate, as though it wanted to escape.

Mrs Cox ate her supper without noticing – all her attention was on her cushion-cover – but Mr Cox tucked into his marrows with relish.

"This is grand!" he told Mallory. "I was born and brought up in the North, Mallory, and this is just the sort of food your granny used to give me when I was your age."

"Didn't she like you?" Mallory asked quietly.

He was trying to work out a way of sneaking his stuffed marrow into a napkin so he could throw

it away later, when suddenly the dining-room door opened and a striking-looking man entered, wearing a long, black cloak and a floppy, black hat. The man had a thin, pointed nose and a white beard that was as bristly as a loo-brush. In one hand, he carried a crystal on a piece of string, and in the other he held what seemed to be a television remote-control unit.

"Good evening!" boomed the stranger. "Allow me to introduce myself. I am Dr Topping, of the Institute for the Investigation of Creepy Goings-On."

"I'm Clive Cox," replied Mr Cox. "This is my wife, Patricia and my son, Mallory."

Dr Topping fixed Mallory with a stare as yellow and hard as an eagle's beak. Mallory felt a cold sensation go down his back and he wiggled uncomfortably in his chair.

"What are those things you're carrying?" he asked.

"This fragment of rock crystal is sensitive to vibrations in mood," said Dr Topping, twirling the string so that the crystal twinkled. "And this little gadget is a Weirdometer. I invented it myself. It picks up the presence of anything unearthly. Nifty isn't it?"

Mallory refused to be impressed.

"Hah and pah!" he scoffed. "You'd better go

somewhere else if you want to investigate creepy goings-on! Nothing strange ever happens in Drab-thorpe!"

Dr Topping narrowed his eyes until they were thinner than five-pence pieces. "Now that's just where you're wrong, Mallory, my boy," he said. "All sorts of peculiar things could happen in a place like this!"

"Coo-er!" gaped Mallory.

He wondered if packing his magic socks had been a waste of time after all. If Dr Topping was right, the holiday in Drabthorpe could turn out to be a lot more exciting than Mallory had expected.

-3-

A Rainy Ramble

Next morning, it was raining. As the Coxes went into the dining-room, they heard drops pattering against the windows and the view outside was as grey and dismal as the inside of Mrs Granite's stuffed marrows.

A few other guests were seated at their tables, glumly chewing their way through breakfast, but there was no sign of Dr Topping.

"Drat and bother!" Mallory said to himself. "I wanted to ask him a lot of nosy questions and have a fiddle about with that Weirdometer."

The family sat down at a table near a window and Mrs Granite popped out of nowhere, wearing a smile as warm as a grandma's hug.

"And what have you got planned today?" she asked brightly. "A stroll along the esplanade?"

"Not in this weather," said Mr Cox.

"It's not very good today, is it?" Mrs Granite said sympathetically. "You should have been here this time last week. There was a magnificent downpour – and it was so cold, we had carol-singers knocking on the door!"

"It's sunny and warm at home," Mrs Cox commented as she worked a needle through her embroidery. "I always think that the best part of a holiday is that it's a change from what you're used to!"

She showed her cushion-cover to Mrs Granite.

"I couldn't get the right shade of blue for the Duke's uniform. Do you think lime-green suits him?"

"It's no good asking me about modern art!"
Mrs Granite declared. "I'll just nip and get you
a hearty, Drabthorpe breakfast."

Breakfast consisted of bowls of porridge, with
lumps round and rubbery enough to use as squash
balls, and kippers that tasted like the insides of run-
ning-shoes. Mallory sipped tea to take away the
taste of the food, and nibbled food to take away
the taste of the tea.

"It's a touch too wet to sit on the beach in
deck-chairs," Mr Cox decided. "I think we should
get togged out in our walking gear and take a ram-
ble up Greezly Tor. There should be a fine view
of the clouds and rain from the top."

After breakfast, Mallory dashed to his room making as much noise as a herd of wild boar playing leap-frog in a piano factory. Half-way up the stairs, Mallory met Dr Topping coming down. Dr Topping was pale and panting and when Mallory said, "Hello there!", the whiskery scientist scowled and muttered something under his breath.

"What's put him in such a bad mood?" wondered Mallory.

But when he got to his room, he found a puzzle that put Dr Topping right out of his thoughts. One of his magic socks was missing. He was sure he had placed both socks inside the sleeve of a sweat-shirt for safe-keeping.

"It must have crawled off somewhere by itself," Mallory decided. "I haven't got time to look for it now. I wonder if one works just as well as a pair?"

He put on his magic sock, made sure it was completely hidden under his walking-boot, and looked eagerly at his reflection in the dressing table mirror. To his disappointment, his hair was its usual mousy colour and the sock didn't feel sparky or tingly, as it would if magic was at work.

"Oh, rotten rats!" said Mallory. "Still, I'd better stuff my head in the balaclava anyway, just to be on the safe side."

Greezly Tor stood in the countryside just outside Drabthorpe. It was a vast, green mound in the shape of a knobbly fist – too tall to be a hill and too small to be a mountain. Mr Cox parked the car at the foot of the tor and the family toiled up the stony track to the top, with cold rain lashing in their faces. Scrawny sheep ran about, frisking and bleating.

"They look happy enough!" Mallory said above the noise of the wind.

"They're the famous Drabthorpe Waterproof Sheep," said Mr Cox. "Their wool is used to make umbrellas."

"I wish my thread was waterproof!" sighed Mrs Cox. "The colours are running. The Princess's face

looks like two currants in a bowl of pink blanc-
mange! I've got no room for my cushion-cover
in this anorak, the pockets are too full of mint
cake."

"I'll take care of it, Mum," Mallory offered,
and he slipped the soggy embroidery inside his
anorak.

The rain stopped as they reached the top, and
the view was bathed in light the colour of steel-
works. The family gazed down on the wet slate
roofs of Drabthorpe and the fields of dripping corn
that surrounded Greezly Tor.

"Tumbling tortoises, look at that!" yelped Mallory.

He pointed to a field where the corn had been

flattened into mysterious-looking circles and lines.

"I wonder what caused that?" mused Mr Cox.

"What indeed, my dear sir!" came a voice from behind.

The Coxes turned and saw Dr Topping, his cloak flapping like a black sail in the wind.
"Some say the marks are the works of practical jokers," Dr Topping went on. "but I'm not so sure."

"Neither am I!" agreed Mallory. "I don't believe anybody who lives in Drabthorpe has a sense of humour!"

He wondered where Dr Topping had appeared from. Surely no one but the Cox family would have even contemplated tackling Greezly Tor in such awful weather.

Dr Topping ignored Mallory's comment.

"I suspect that the marks are made by alien visitors, who are attempting to . . ."

He broke off as his Weirdometer began to make pipping, bleeping noises. Dr Topping looked at it with bulging eyes.

"Einstein's eyebrows, what's happening?" he gasped. "My Weirdometer has gone completely wacky! Something unearthly must be going on close-by!"

Mallory stared with a puzzled expression at Dr Topping, whose hair had started to turn green.

He was just going to ask about this, when he felt something happening. His right foot felt like it was filling up with fizzy treacle and he guessed that his magic sock was doing its stuff. It must have turned multi-coloured, for tiny rainbows were shining out of his lace-holes and pale-blue steam was rising from his heel.

The sock was doing more than making the Weirdometer react. Mallory's mouth fell wide open as a large object rose up behind Greezly Tor and hovered directly overhead.

~4~

An Alien Ambush

The object was made of silvery metal and was shaped like two enormous saucepan-lids stuck together top-to-bottom. Round windows around the sides flashed different colours, and Mallory noticed that they matched exactly the lights coming out of his lace-holes – right down to the last flicker.

"Mallory!" thundered Mr Cox. "You've got your magic socks on again, haven't you?"

"That's only half-true, Dad," Mallory confessed meekly.

"I've told you time and time again that you are not to wear those socks outside the house!" Mr Cox stormed, against the sound of the howling wind and the engines of the alien spacecraft.

Dr Topping barged into the conversation, waving his arms wildly.

"My dear Mr Cox," he said angrily, "this is

no time to discuss hosiery! We're having a close encounter!"

"Yes, Clive," agreed Mrs Cox, "and it would make a lovely design for an embroidered table-cloth!"

The spacecraft gave off an uncanny, whistling hum and Mallory's sock responded with a quieter version of the same noise. Mallory's foot had never been inside a hum before – it made his toe-nails tickle. He was beginning to feel extremely lopsided too, and he wondered regretfully about the whereabouts of his missing sock.

"Never mind embroidered table-cloths and phooey to close encounters!" raged Mr Cox. "Mallory, get those socks off at once before something dangerous happens!"

But Mr Cox's warning came too late. As Mallory crouched down to untie his boot-lace, a beam of violet light shone out of the spacecraft and surrounded him. Mallory suddenly felt as light and bubbly as a milk-shake, and before he knew what was happening, he rose gently into the air.

"Hang on tightly, Mallory!" shouted Mr Cox.

"But there's nothing to hang on to!" Mallory wailed.

Dr Topping gave a cry as a second light appeared around him and he too was lifted up towards the glittering spaceship.

"They never told me about this sort of thing at the Institute!" he grunted. "Scary, isn't it?"

Mallory glanced downwards to see his parents racing about like waterproof sheep, shouting things that he couldn't hear. When he looked above, he saw that a door had opened in the bright metal and the violet lights were drawing him and Dr Topping towards the yawning doorway.

"Stand by, dear boy!" bawled Dr Topping. "I believe they're going to take us on board!"

It felt exactly the same as falling, only travelling up instead of down. Mallory closed his eyes and waited for the almighty thump he was sure would come. But instead of being bashed and battered, he simply stopped moving. There was solid floor under his feet.

"We're there, lad!" croaked Dr Topping. "We've been ambushed by aliens, and now we're actually inside a vehicle from another world!"

Mallory opened his eyes cautiously. The inside of the spaceship looked awful. The floor was covered with a tatty, green carpet and the walls were covered with dark-red, furry paper patterned in gold. Pale-blue pipes ran across the yellow ceiling.

"Yu-kky!" exclaimed Mallory.

"This ship was built by beings whose intelligence must be far greater than our own!" said Dr Topping hoarsely. "Just think of it – an advanced race with incredibly poor taste in interior decoration!"

The doctor adjusted his hat and cleared his throat. A strange shifty look glinted in his eyes.

"Did I, er, hear your father mention that your socks are magic?" he asked casually.

"That's right," said Mallory.

"Of course, as a scientist I don't believe in any mumbo-jumbo, superstitious nonsense about magic!" laughed Dr Topping nervously. "But, er, purely in the interests of science, why don't you take them off and let me examine them?"

"Certainly not!" said Mallory. "We're in enough trouble as it is, without you messing about with my socks!"

"Just lift up the right leg of your jeans so I can take a peek at the other one, then!" begged Dr Topping. "Go on, don't be a meanie!"

Before Mallory could demand exactly what Dr Topping meant by "the other one", there was a sound like a saucepan filled with pins coming to the boil. Mallory frowned deeply, then frowned more deeply still as he realised that the sound was a voice, and that the magic in his socks was helping him to understand what the voice was saying.

"So, the plan was successful! Set course for the planet Groxx at once!"

-5-

A Proper Pickle

Mallory wheeled around so quickly that his glasses nearly fell off. A round door had opened in one of the walls, and in the doorway stood an alien.

Its head was rather like a rabbit's, with long, furry ears but instead of a rabbit's nose, it had a trunk that dangled down to its neck. The alien's body was human-shaped and dressed in what appeared to be a baggy shell-suit made from cooking foil.

"Who are you?" demanded Mallory.

The alien was so surprised that its ears curled up until they looked like pancake rolls.

"So, you speak Groxxish!" it said. "This will make communication far easier. My name is Venki. I'm pleased to meet you."

Mallory didn't bother to explain that he couldn't

speak Groxxish and that it was the magic in his socks playing tricks, he just said, "I'm Mallory Cox and this is Dr Topping and we're not sure if we're pleased to meet you or not."

He turned to Dr Topping.

"He says his name is – "

"I understood, no need to translate, dear boy!" declared Dr Topping.

Mallory frowned suspiciously as he wondered how it could be that Dr Topping spoke an alien language, but more urgent matters drove the thought from his mind.

"Let us off this ship at once!" Mallory demanded. "My parents are bound to make a fuss

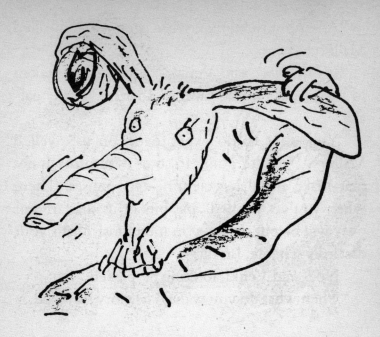

because we'll be late for lunch at Mrs Granite's!"

Venki unrolled one of his ears and scratched it with a paw.

"Not possible," he said. "Spaceship Seven is now travelling at top speed towards our home planet, Groxx. Even if it could turn round, it's travelling so fast that if we returned to earth, we would probably land long before we left – possibly in a time before you were born."

If Mallory could have curled up his ears, he would certainly have done so, "Eh?" he squeaked.

"Special Theory of Relativity, old chap," murmured Dr Topping. "I'll explain it to you when you've got a couple of weeks to spare."

"All I want to know is what's going on!" shrilled Mallory.

"It's simple," said Venki. "You're being taken to the planet Groxx, on the other side of the galaxy."

"You want to do experiments on us!" yelled Mallory. "You're going to strap us into machines that make peculiar, scientific-type noises! Then, when you've finished, any bits of us that are left over will be put on show in museums! That's your dastardly scheme, isn't it?"

"No," said Venki, looking perplexed.

"Then what do you want?" Mallory shrieked.

"We want you to tell us some jokes," said Venki.

Mallory was so astonished that he sat cross-legged on the tacky, green carpet.

"Jokes?" he boggled. "What on earth — I mean — why do you want me to tell you jokes?"

"On Groxx, all the jokes have been used up," explained Venki. "We've heard them all so many times that they don't make us laugh any more. We've spent so much time being serious, studying science and building complicated machines that we forgot about laughter and now we've lost it. We want it back again."

Mallory removed his glasses and his balaclava helmet so that he could scratch his head. His magic sock had turned the right side of his hair Cheddar-cheese coloured.

"What makes you think I can help?" he asked.

Venki curled his trunk behind his left ear.

"But ... you told the computer you could!" he said in a puzzled voice. "It was programmed to seek out the funniest being in the galaxy. It scanned you with fact-collecting beams, and you're just what we've been looking for."

"Hang on!" groaned Mallory as a thought struck him. "Are you talking about the lights that came out of the ship before you grabbed us?"

"Of course," replied Venki.

Mallory remembered the matching coloured lights coming from his magic sock and moaned.

"Drat and dash!" he grumbled. "It's all the fault of my witchy Great Aunt and her bothersome birthday present! My sock has got me into a proper pickle this time! I'm going to stay here on the floor and have a fit of the sulks. I don't want to be disturbed!"

–6–

Bubble and Banquet

By the time Mallory had finished his sulk, Spaceship Seven was circling the planet Groxx. It was an orange and blue planet, striped with bands of white cloud which looked like layers of cream in a cake. Mallory and Dr Topping stared at it from one of the windows.

"Another world, dear boy!" Dr Topping said grandly. "And we're the first humans ever to set eyes on it. It makes me feel very humble!"

"I don't feel anything except hungry!" groused Mallory. "I could even eat a Drabthorpe delicacy – well, a bit of one, anyway!"

"You'll be having a feast, soon," Venki informed him. "We have already broadcast the news of our success to the Great Council. A banquet is being prepared in the Hall of Fame. We're going straight there after we've landed."

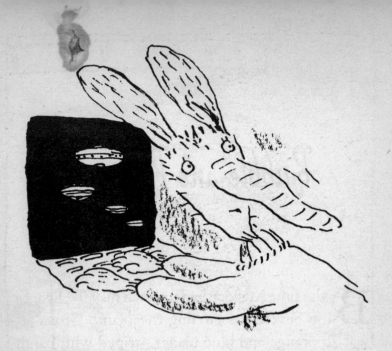

"When will that be?" snapped Mallory. "My stomach is making noises like a hippo in a mud wallow!"

"Unfortunately there will be a slight delay," said Venki. "So many Groxxians are flying in to catch a sight of you that we're in the middle of a long queue of ships."

"A traffic jam!" fumed Mallory. "I've travelled from one end of the galaxy to the other, just to get stuck in a blooming traffic jam!"

"Patience, old thing!" Dr Topping advised. "Better polish up your funny bone while we're waiting – get a few rib-tickling quips ready to amuse our hosts. That is, if they have ribs."

"Hmm!" said Mallory, quietly.

Secretly Mallory was thinking that the Groxxian computer must have made a big mistake. Mallory didn't believe that he was the funniest being in the galaxy — in fact, he knew hardly any jokes. He was more interested in showing-off his knowledge of mind-bogglingly useless facts than making people laugh. His only hope was that his magic sock would help him to come up with something.

After what seemed like ages, Spaceship Seven landed. Venki led Mallory and Dr Topping down a ramp to where a large bubble was parked. It turned out to be the Groxxian version of a taxi. Mallory followed Venki and stepped through the bubble wall – it felt like taking a bath in tapioca pudding.

Although the bubble had no engine and no driver, it seemed to know where it was going. When all three of its passengers were inside, it shot into the air and whizzed along, flying above a city of huge buildings shaped like pyramids and cubes.

"Just think!" exclaimed Dr Topping. "Only an incredibly thin layer of atoms is keeping us from falling to our doom! Spooky, isn't it?"

"I've been on fairground rides far scarier than this," said Mallory, pretending not to be frightened – but half his hair turned the colour of liquorice

allsorts as the bubble fell at terrific speed towards a large, dome-shaped building. "We're going to be mashed into mango chutney!" he screeched. "If I ever get back home, I'm never going to wear my mankey magic socks again!"

"Really?" said Dr Topping. "Would you consider donating them to the Institute for Investigation?"

Mallory glared at him.

The bubble hurtled into a hole in the side of the building, zoomed along a dark passage and burst with a loud PLOOT leaving its passengers standing on a raised platform at one end of an enormous room. The walls were decorated in a ghastly flower-pattern and frilly curtains hung at the gigantic windows. Seated at long tables were crowds of Groxxians, all staring expectantly at the newcomers.

Mallory had thought that all the inhabitants of Groxx would look like Venki – now he realised that Venki was one of the better-looking Groxxians. Some had squid-like tentacles on their faces, some had two heads and some had long teeth as curved as wart-hog tusks.

"Don't they look fascinating?" whispered Dr Topping. "So different from us! So unusual! So hideously ugly!"

A Groxxian wearing a badly-made puce suit,

who had white fur on all three of his cabbage-leaf shaped ears, stood up and began to make a speech.

"Welcome to the Hall of Fame! This is indeed an historic moment. Our long quest is over. Soon, the Groxxians will be given back the precious gift of laughter. But first, let us eat – and in celebration of this momentous occasion, the first course will be thrub soup!"

In the excited murmur that followed this announcement, Mallory and the others made their way to a table set for three. Mallory sat down and a dish like a goldfish bowl was set in front of him. The bowl was filled with a steaming liquid that looked like river mud mixed with wet leaves.

"Thrub soup!" said Venki, obviously delighted. "I haven't had any thrub soup since the last time I had some!"

"How do we eat it?" Mallory whispered nervously to Dr Topping. "We haven't got any spoons!"

"Just watch carefully and do what Venki does, old son!" Dr Topping advised.

Venki folded his ears back behind his head, thrust his trunk deep into his bowl and made a noise like a sink being unblocked. He finished his soup and looked surprised when he saw that Mallory's bowl was still full.

"Don't you like it?" he asked.

"Um, I seem to have lost my appetite," fibbed Mallory. "It must be all the excitement."

The soup was followed by something that looked like a withered gherkin in raspberry sauce, and then a plate of greenish, custardy stuff that twitched. There were a dozen other courses even more disgusting-looking. Mallory couldn't face any of them – nor could Dr Topping.

"Tell me, Mallory, old sport," the doctor murmured, "can't you use magic to get us out of here? Or at least rustle us up some decent grub?"

"I've got no control over my socks," said Mallory. "They only work when they want to, and at the moment they don't seem to want to … anyway, I only have one of them on."

There was no more time for questions – the puce-suited Groxxian had stood up again.

"Before I introduce our honoured guest," he said, "I think it's time I told him about one of our quaint Groxxian customs. Those guests who please us are rewarded beyond their wildest dreams; but guests who fail to please us are given to … the Snarkler!"

At that instant a door at the back of the hall crashed open and a savage-looking creature bounded in. It was restrained by six Groxxians who hung on to an enormous leash.

The creature was like a black ink-blot, except

that no ink–blot Mallory had ever seen before had
a huge red mouth with vicious fangs.

"What's that?" he whimpered.

"The Snarkler," said Venki. "But there's no
need to worry, the computer picked you, so the
poor beast will go hungry today!"

"I wouldn't be so sure!" Mallory croaked.

The Groxxian in puce pointed to Mallory.

"Will you put your paws together, please, and
welcome our very special guest ... the funniest
being in the galaxy – Mallory Cox!"

"Petrified prunes!" quailed Mallory, staring at
the Snarkler's slavering jaws. "I wish I'd left both
my stupid socks at home!"

Groxxian Giggles

Reluctantly Mallory rose to his feet as the furry applause died down.

"Er, hello there!" he said nervously. "I'd like to say thanks a lot for the delicious banquet – but I can't, because I didn't eat any of it! Ha, ha!"

There was a restless shuffling around the hall and Mallory could tell that his speech wasn't going down too well. The Snarkler licked its lips with a red tongue the size of a bathtowel. Mallory's blood ran cold.

"Um ... here's a joke I read in a Christmas cracker," he quaked. "Christmas crackers are quite popular on earth. They're sort of crackers that we have when it's Christmas. Well, here goes: what's the longest word in the English language?"

The Groxxians didn't even try to guess at the answer, they just went on staring.

"Smiles!" Mallory said triumphantly. "Because there's a mile between the first and last letters!"

For a moment there was absolute silence, and then, to Mallory's delight, he heard the sound of laughter, wheezier than a bear inflating a balloon. His joy vanished quickly, however, when he discovered that the laugh came from Dr Topping, and that he was the only one laughing.

"Smiles, eh? What a card the boy is!" the doctor guffawed, elbowing Venki in the side. Venki didn't even smile a little bit.

"How about this one, then?" said Mallory. "I got it from an old comic. Where do owls stay when they go on holiday? In a hoot-el!"

Dr Topping laughed until he was red in the face. He was a very good actor, but even so none of the Groxxians were joining in.

Mallory was red in the face, too, but not from laughter. He was blushing with embarrassment. It suddenly seemed extremely warm in the Hall of Fame. Mallory felt sweat trickling down his face and decided to take off his anorak. As he unzipped it, Mrs Cox's embroidered cushion-cover fell out on to the floor.

"Just the job for giving my face a quick wipe!" Mallory muttered as he bent down to rescue it.

He unfolded the cushion-cover and mopped his brow with it, realising as he did so that his store of jokes was used up.

But something was happening. The Groxxians were waggling their ears furiously and their trunks were tying themselves into knots. They doubled over, squeaking like rusty bicycle-wheels, and fell off their chairs. The Snarkler was rolling on its back making gargling noises.

"Are you feeling ill?" enquired Mallory. "I thought that thrub soup looked a bit off!"

"They're not ill, old dear!" grinned Dr Topping. "They're laughing! You've done it! Quick, think of some more jokes!"

"No!" Venki gasped from the floor. "It isn't the jokes that are making us laugh! It's that thing he's holding!"

"What, this?" said Mallory, waving the cushion-cover about. As he did so, the Groxxians redoubled their squeaking and the Snarkler had to be carried helpless from the hall.

"But this is Mum's embroidery! Her pride and joy! Her present for the Palace! It's a picture of the royal family!" Mallory said indignantly. "It's terribly bad manners to laugh at the royal family!"

The Groxxians didn't think so, and the more Mallory complained and waved the cushion-cover about, the more they hooted and giggled.

The Groxxian in the puce suit staggered across the hall, took the cushion-cover from Mallory's hands and held it high.

"Now we have this, we need never be miserable again!" he announced. "We'll build a factory to produce these by the million, and then if we feel the need for a quick snigger, all we'll have to do is take a look. I declare Mallory Cox to be a Groxxian hero and later on I shall present him with a Golden Trunk award."

"Lolloping llamas!" Mallory said proudly. "And the magic socks didn't do anything to rescue me! I did it all by myself – with a bit help of help from Mum. So I don't need magic to help me out of nasty scrapes!"

He turned to Dr Topping to tell him all about it, but the doctor was in no state to listen to any-

thing. He was spinning round slowly, like a round-about starting up.

"Hey!" gasped Mallory. "Why are coloured lights coming out of your left boot? And why are you starting to fade? If I didn't know better, I'd say that – "

There was no time to puzzle it out. Deep inside Mallory's walking-boot, something stirred. Magic was sizzling between his toes and around his ankle.

The hall and the Groxxians began to melt away like candy-floss and Mallory felt himself twirling like a twig in a whirlpool.

"Oh dear!" he cried. "I think my sock is at it again!"

-8-

An Unscrupulous Great Uncle

It was the worst journey Mallory's magic socks had ever given him. He was swallowed by green spirals and spun around until he was giddy. Lights burst in front of his eyes with the brightness of exploding fireworks and his ears were deafened by a screeching as loud as tigers sharpening their claws on the side of a tank.

Just when Mallory thought that he couldn't bear any more, the lights stopped and he saw a misty picture of his parents on top of Greezly Tor. The picture grew clearer by the second. Mallory landed with his legs twisted round like a corkscrew.

"So there you are, Mallory!" seethed Mr Cox. "Do you realise you've kept us waiting here for more than half an hour? Your mother and I have been frantic with worry and ..."

Mallory wasn't listening, he was staring in

69

amazement at Dr Topping. The doctor had lost his floppy hat along the way, and the left side of his hair was purple and sparkling. His beard was dangling from one side of his face like an exhausted Persian cat.

"Just a tick!" Mallory said suspiciously. He reached up and pulled the beard off. It was made from frayed rope.

Without his beard, Dr Topping looked completely different. The tip of his nose almost touched the point of his bony chin and his eyes lurked under their bushy brows like timid wood lice.

"I know you!" gasped Mr Cox. "You're Great Aunt Enid's brother, Great Uncle Oliver!"

"Fiddlesticks!" cursed Great Uncle Oliver. "Foiled by a pot of dodgy beard-glue!"

"Are you a bit on the witchy side, like my Great Aunts?" asked Mallory.

"No, I'm on the wizardly side!" scowled Great Uncle Oliver. "I was never as clever at magic as our Enid because I'm too soft-hearted. That's why I wanted your magic socks, lad. I could do a lot of good about the place if I got my tootsies inside them both!"

"You pinched one of my socks!" spluttered Mallory, suddenly realising what had been going on. "That was why you were taken to Groxx with me and how you were able to understand Groxxian

71

when you got there! Of all the low-down, sneaky, under-handed tricks!"

"Thanks," smiled Great Uncle Oliver. "It was a cracking bit of wickedness, but my heart wasn't really in it. Not my style, you see I suppose you'd better have your sock back now the game's up!"

Mr Cox had been listening with folded arms and a tapping foot, but he suddenly unfolded his arms and clicked his fingers.

"I've got a much better idea!" he declared. "Mallory, this magic sock nonsense has gone on quite long enough. Take off your sock and give it to your Great Uncle!"

"What?" gasped Mallory.

"Better do as your father says, dear," whispered Mrs Cox. "I've never seen him look so firm – it quite suits him!"

Mallory sat down on the wet grass and unlaced his boot.

"Oh, all right then!" he said grumpily.

"You've always been a bit of a show-off and a know-it-all, Mallory," said Mr Cox. "I was hoping you might grow out of it, but I'm afraid those socks have only made you worse! If you don't get rid of them, you'll never make friends or have fun!"

The magic sock was ordinary-looking again. Mallory peeled it off with a sigh.

"Oh, hump and ha!" he groused. "This means I'll have to be like other kids and do things like play football and go to discos instead of having magical shenanigans!"

"And a good thing too!" sighed Mr Cox.

Mallory held out the sock to Great Uncle Oliver. It stood upright on his palm, tapped its heel, piped, "Yippee!" and leapt into the wizard's outstretched hand.

"You've made the right decision, lad," said Great Uncle Oliver, slipping off his right boot and slipping on the magic sock. "I'll make sure they're used for a worthwhile cause. Well, I'd better be toddling along to my cave in the moors – my cat will want feeding. Bye for now. I'll drop you a postcard when I get a moment!"

The wizard spread his arms and flew off into the grey sky, trailing showers of flamingo-coloured sparks.

"That's that!" sighed Mallory. "No more dangerous magical adventures . . . no more alien spacecraft, no more demented dinosaurs, no more being whisked about through time and space . . ."

He tried to be regretful, but the more he thought about his socks, the more relieved he felt that they had gone.

"Thank goodness!" he breathed.

He remembered the cushion-cover and turned to his mother.

"Sorry, Mum," he apologised. "your embroidery got lost on my enchanted escapade."

"Never mind, Mallory," said Mrs Cox as she helped him to his feet. "I was bored with sewing anyway. I think I'll take up knitting instead."

Mallory went pale.

"You can knit me anything you like," he told his mother, "mittens, scarves, jumpers – I'll wear them whatever colour you choose, only . . ."

"Only what, dear?" smiled Mrs Cox.

"Promise you'll never knit me any socks!" Mallory pleaded.

Andrew Matthews

MALLORY COX AND HIS MAGIC SOCKS

Mallory Cox is a know-it-all and a show off!
Mallory thinks he knows *everything* – until
the day Great Aunt Enid from up North flies
in with a very bewitching birthday present.
Then he finds he's got a thing or two to learn
about some of his relatives who are a bit on
the witchy side, and in the meantime he's
caught right in the middle of a huge family
feud. As a result, Mallory has a truly
monstrous adventure and gets his
comeuppance!

With hilarious illustrations by Tony Ross,
this first Mallory Cox Adventure is a
riveting tale of warring witches and
spellbinding socks.

Andrew Matthews

MALLORY COX AND THE VIKING BOX

Mallory Cox's life has not been the same since his witchy Great Aunt gave him a pair of magic socks . . . when he puts them on anything can happen!

When Mallory visits the local museum one day things take a very tricky turn. Before he knows it he's heaving-ho with a bunch of niffy Norsemen, eating foul-smelling fish soup with Freya the Slayer and being chased by a very vicious-looking Viking! How can he get out of this one?

The hilarious sequel to *Mallory Cox and his Magic Socks*.

David Tinkler

REVENGE OF THE DINNER LADIES

Are the Dinner Ladies at your school rough and tough? Do they get into deadly strops? Do they pour vats of hot soup over innocent children? It was exactly the same at Littlebampton Primary where Plughole, the proud owner of the World's Weirdest Laugh, went to school. But when the Dinner Ladies turned up at his home, it was no laughing matter . . .

This is the third story in David Tinkler's hilarious series, following *The Scourge of the Dinner Ladies* and *The Dinner Ladies Clean Up!*

Peter Rowan

PINCH YOUR NOSE AND TRY TO HUM

What are eyebrows for?
Why doesn't your stomach digest itself?
When you take paracetamol for a pain, how
does it know where to go?

This collection of questions sent to Doctor
Peter Rowan's column in the *Early Times*
includes the serious, the funny and the
bizarre. Dr Pete's replies, full of strange facts
and stories, make essential reading for
anyone fascinated by the workings of the
human body.